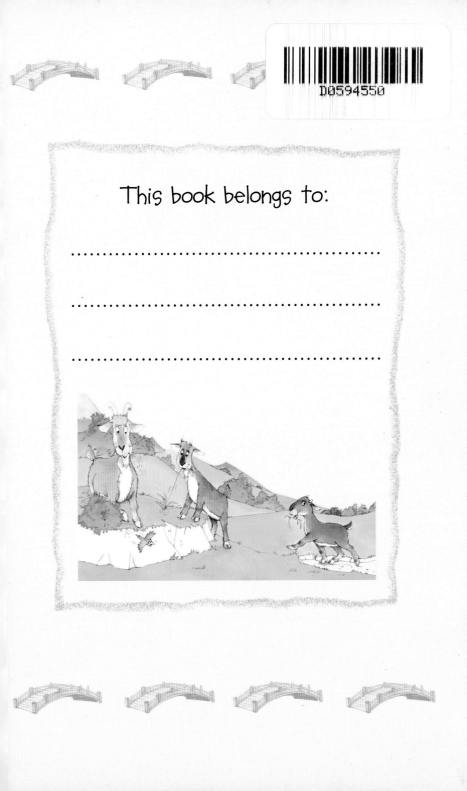

This book belongs to:

....

....

....

Retold by Gaby Goldsack
Illustrated by Kim Blundell (John Martin & Artists)
Designed by Jester Designs

Language consultant: Betty Root

ISBN 0-75259-432-X

This is a P³ book
This edition published in 2002

P³
Queen Street House
4 Queen Street
Bath BA1 1HE, UK
Copyright © Exclusive Editions 2002

Printed in China.

All rights reserved. No part of this publication may be reproduced,
stored in a retrieval system, or transmitted by any means,
mechanical, photocopying, recording, or otherwise, without
the prior permission of the copyright holder.

p^3

The Three Billy Goats Gruff

Helping Your Child Read

Learning to read is an exciting challenge for most children. From a very early age, sharing storybooks with children, talking about the pictures, and guessing what might happen next are all very important parts of the reading experience.

Sharing Reading

Set aside a regular quiet time to share reading with younger children, or to be available to encourage older children as they develop into independent readers.

First Readers are intended to encourage and support the early stages of learning to read. They present well-loved tales that children will enjoy hearing again and again. Familiarity helps children identify some of the words and phrases.

When you feel your child is ready to move ahead, encourage him or her to join in so that you read the story aloud together. Always pause to talk about the pictures. The easy-to-read speech bubbles in **First Readers** provide an excellent "joining-in" activity. The bright, clear illustrations and matching text will help children understand the story.

Building Confidence

In time, children will want to read *to* you. When this happens, be patient and give continual praise. They may not read all the words correctly, but children's substitutions are often very good guesses.

The repetition in each book is especially helpful for building confidence. If your child cannot read a particular word, go back to the beginning of the sentence and read it together so the meaning is not lost. Most importantly, do not continue if your child is tired or just needs a change.

Reading Alone

The next step is for your child to read alone. Try to be available to give help and support. Remember to give lots of encouragement and praise.

Along with other simple stories, **First Readers** will help ensure reading is an enjoyable and rewarding experience for children.

Once upon a time there were three Billy Goats Gruff.

There was a big Billy Goat Gruff.

There was a middle-sized Billy Goat Gruff.

And there was a little Billy Goat Gruff.

The three goats all loved to eat grass.

All day long they ate grass on the hill.
But they never crossed the bridge to eat
the grass on the other side.

They never crossed the bridge because the Troll lived under the bridge.

The Troll was very bad. He ate anyone who dared to cross his bridge.

One day the little Billy Goat Gruff looked at the green, green grass on the other side of the bridge.

"I'm not scared of a silly old Troll," he said. "I'm going to cross the bridge."

"So am I," said the middle-sized Billy Goat Gruff.

"And so am I," said the big Billy Goat Gruff.

I'm not scared.

"You go first. It was your idea," said the big Billy Goat Gruff to the little Billy Goat Gruff.

Trip, trap, trip, trip, trap!

So the little Billy Goat Gruff set off across the bridge.

Trip, trap, trip, trip, trap went his hooves.

"Who is that trip-trapping over my bridge?" roared the Troll.

"It's only me!" said the little Billy Goat Gruff. "I'm going to eat the green, green grass on the other side of the bridge."

"Oh no, you're not!" roared the Troll. "I'm going to eat you up!"

"But I am just little," said the little Billy Goat Gruff. "Wait until my middle-sized brother comes across. He is much bigger than me."

"Very well!" said the Troll.

So the little Billy Goat Gruff crossed the bridge. Soon he was eating the green, green grass.

Next, the middle-sized Billy Goat Gruff crossed the bridge.

"Who is that trip-trapping over my bridge?" roared the Troll.

"It's only me!" said the middle-sized Billy Goat Gruff. "I am going to eat the green, green grass on the other side of the bridge."

"Oh no, you're not!" roared the Troll. "I'm going to eat you up!"

I'm going to eat you up!

"But I am just middle-sized," said the middle-sized Billy Goat Gruff. "Wait until my big brother comes across. He is much bigger than me."

"Very well!" said the Troll.

And don't come back!

So the middle-sized Billy Goat Gruff
crossed the bridge. Soon he was eating
the green, green grass.

Next the big Billy Goat Gruff crossed
the bridge.

Quake! Shake! Rumble!

"Who is that trip-trapping over my
bridge?" roared the Troll.

"It's only me!" said the big Billy Goat Gruff. "I'm going to eat the green, green grass on the other side of the bridge."

"Oh no, you're not!" roared the Troll. "I'm going to eat you up!"

The Troll jumped onto the bridge.

The big Billy Goat Gruff lowered his horns and charged.

Crash! The big Billy Goat Gruff banged into the Troll. The Troll flew into the air. Splash! He fell into the water.

Take that!

Crash!
Splash!

The big Billy Goat Gruff skipped over the bridge. Soon he was eating the green, green grass.

And the ugly Troll was never seen again.

Hooray!

Read and Say

How many of these words can you say?
The pictures will help you. Look back in
your book and see if you can find the
words in the story.

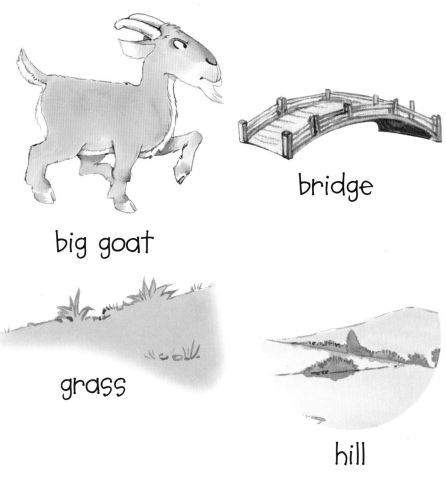

bridge

big goat

grass

hill

hooves

horns

little goat

middle-sized goat

Troll

water